Aimee and Divine Inspiration

On a Journey

Michaela
Shine your light !!

Diane Bourgeois

Diane Bourgeois
Love
C

Balboa Press books may be ordered through booksellers or by contacting:

Balboa Press
A Division of Hay House
1663 Liberty Drive
Bloomington, IN 47403
www.balboapress.com
1 (877) 407-4847

Because of the dynamic nature of the Internet, any web addresses or links contained in this book may have changed since publication and may no longer be valid. The views expressed in this work are solely those of the author and do not necessarily reflect the views of the publisher, and the publisher hereby disclaims any responsibility for them.

Any people depicted in stock imagery provided by Thinkstock are models, and such images are being used for illustrative purposes only.
Certain stock imagery © Thinkstock.

ISBN: 978-1-5043-5745-6 (sc)
ISBN: 978-1-5043-5746-3 (e)

Library of Congress Control Number: 2016907298

Print information available on the last page.

Balboa Press rev. date: 06/10/2016

BALBOA
PRESS
A DIVISION OF HAY HOUSE

To my beloved mother, who passed away in 2012

The lessons she taught me about connecting with the Great Spirit and respecting Mother Earth have brought me to a place of love and gratitude. In times of great change, I honor the people of different tribes around the world who are awakening to their power as creators of the New Earth.

A prophecy from the Native American Hopi tribe inspired Aimee, a young North American girl, to heal Mother Earth.

In a dream, an elder spoke to her and said, "When the earth is dying, there shall arise a new tribe of all colors and all creeds. This tribe shall be called the Warriors of the Rainbow, and it will put its faith in actions, not words."

Aimee, a member of this tribe of many colors, decided to go on an adventure to discover her true nature.

Aimee is excited to begin her new journey with her boat, *Divine Inspiration*, who represents the guiding light of her soul.

Aimee boarded her boat, *Divine Inspiration*.

Divine Inspiration asked, "What's in your bag?"

Aimee replied, "Clothes, a first-aid kit, and my blankie named Shima."

Divine Inspiration asked, "Are you ready to go?"

Aimee replied, "I'm ready!"

As they cruised along on the river, Aimee saw a waterfall ahead.

Divine Inspiration whispered, "See the beauty of the falls."

Aimee said, "I see it."

Aimee approached the waterfall and asked *Divine Inspiration*, "What's that?"

"It's an opening to another world. Mother Earth is revealing the stargate of your life. How do you feel?" *Divine Inspiration* asked.

"I feel confident in my journey. Thank you, Mother Earth," Aimee said. "What is happening to me?"

"You are experiencing your life purpose," replied *Divine Inspiration*.

Captivated by the vision, Aimee drifted into a daydream.

After leaving the waterfall, Aimee said, "Look! There's an island up ahead! Help me find a good place to anchor."

"Try that beach near the middle of the island," *Divine Inspiration* replied.

"Get closer to the shore so you don't have to swim," *Divine Inspiration* said.

"Thanks!" Aimee replied.

Aimee explored the island and noticed something glittering in the woods. "I am not alone!" She ran toward the glittering forest.

Aimee had fun playing, laughing, and dancing with the fairies of the forest.

Aimee saw a beautiful fairy wearing a sapphire dress, and she wondered who could it be.

"Who are you?" she asked.

"I am Krystal Sapphire, the fairy grandmother and wisdom keeper here to teach you how to live in the heart."

"I am on a quest to learn how to have a balanced relationship with Mother Earth," Aimee said.

"You are on the right path to remember who you are," Krystal Sapphire replied.

"How do you survive in the woods?" Aimee asked Krystal Sapphire, the fairy grandmother.

"The forest gives us food, medicine, and shelter. We can help you gather what you need for the night," Krystal Sapphire said.

"Thank you for your help," Aimee said.

Krystal Sapphire replied, "You're welcome. We are here to help you connect with the beauty of the forest."

Seeing a shooting star, Aimee said silently, "Help me connect with my soul family." She then realized she could create anything she wanted as long as she had joy in her heart.

The next day, Aimee and *Divine Inspiration* sailed down the river to a new place.

Grandmother Spirit whispered, "You walk the path of the ancient ones. Remember that this is not your home."

Aimee replied, "I want to help others and spread joy."

Grandmother Spirit whispered, "Mother Nature is your calling. The stars are within you, not outside of you."

Aimee listened to Grandmother Spirit, the elder in her previous dream. She returned to her journey on the river of life.

The river flowed in the direction of a dark cave.

"I am scared!" Aimee said.

"Fear is like a bad dream. Once you follow your heart, it guides you to safety," *Divine Inspiration* replied.

"May I ask for help?" Aimee asked.

"Yes! The angels of light are here to guide you," answered *Divine Inspiration*.

They both lit up their stars of joy within their heart flames.

"I am thinking with my heart. Look! The shadows are running away from the light!" exclaimed Aimee.

"Only love can drive out the shadows. Trust the love," said *Divine Inspiration*.

"I made it!" exclaimed Aimee.

"Love conquers everything," *Divine Inspiration* replied.

"I could hear the energy of Grandmother Spirit in my heart," Aimee said.

"The energy of the inner voice flows through the heart to create little miracles," *Divine Inspiration* exclaimed.

"What does a miracle look like?" Aimee asked.

Divine Inspiration smiled. "It looks like little sparkles of light with many colors."

Looking ahead, Aimee asked, "Is that what you mean?"

Divine Inspiration replied, "Let's go see."

As they got closer, Divine Inspiration said, "I can glide toward the Rainbow Bridge. Do you hear the whispering?"

Aimee replied, "No. What do you hear?"

Divine Inspiration said, "Open yourself to the Great Spirit. It will guide you."

"I am changing. Fear is gone. The Rainbow Bridge of Love brings me joy," Aimee said.

"We're all sparks of the Creative Force," *Divine Inspiration* replied.

After her beautiful experience, Aimee heard a whisper in the wind, "Cosmic love is where the Great Spirit speaks. Honor the eternal starlight within. Spread love and gratitude everywhere you go. Love yourself, as you are the stewards of Mother Earth!"

Aimee waved good-bye to her old ways.

Divine Inspiration said, "Look at the sky. What do you see?"

Aimee replied, "A huge rainbow encircling the sun. Does it have a name?"

Divine Inspiration replied, "It's called a sun dog. It is a message from the Great Spirit. Once the rainbow encircles each person's heart, all will remember Mother Earth."

Aimee nodded and exclaimed, "I am light! It is the path of the heart to remember the joyful blessings of the Great Spirit and Creator in returning Mother Earth to beauty."

About the Author

Diane Bourgeois has had psychic experiences for as long as she can remember. She lives every day according to her personal mantra: love, play, and create value for others.

Diane devotes her free time to practicing meditation at home and in nature, engaging in the intuitive arts, writing and inspired by nature. Diane lives in Gatineau Quebec, Canada.

You can reach her at divinenotebook@wordpress.com.

About the Book

Will Aimee find her true self in her darkest hour? Will Aimee get lost in the shadow cave? Follow Aimee on the river of change as she goes into a forest of dreams and ventures through the cave of shadows. Will Aimee be brave enough to find her rainbow?

This book is about a child on a quest to discover her true self. The divine river of life takes her on a journey of great change through magical forests of strength and love. On her voyage, the cave of shadows challenges her. If she can pass through the cave, she will discover the greatest treasure of her life!

CPSIA information can be obtained
at www.ICGtesting.com
Printed in the USA
LVHW07s1739150618
580804LV00003B/4/P